HEY JACQUES, LET'S GO TO THE CAFÉ.

COLOR SEPARATIONS BY IMAGO LTD, HONG KONG

PRINTED IN HONG KONG BY SOUTH CHINA PRINTING CO.

DESIGNE

PUBLISHED BY
THE PENGUIN GROUP
VIKING PENGUIN INC.
375 HUDSON ST. NY NY 10014
PENGUIN BOOKS LTD.
27 WRIGHTS LANE
LONDON W8 5TZ ENGLAND
PENGUIN BOOKS AUSTRALIA LTD.
RINGWOOD, VICTORIA, AUSTRALIA
PENGUIN BOOKS CANADA LTD.
10 ALCORN AVENUE
TORONTO, ONTARIO, CANADA M4V 3B2
PENGUIN BOOKS (N.Z.) LTD.
182-190 WAIRAU RD.
AUCKLAND 10, NEW ZEALAND
PENGUIN BOOKS LTD,
REGISTERED OFFICES:
HARMONDSWORTH,
MIDDLESEX, ENGLAND

SPECIAL WILLY THANKS TO K-K- KIKA

AND ALWAYS AND FOREVER TO MR. TIBOR AND DOS LOCOS BAMBINOS CON TODO MI AMOR

LIBRARY OF CONGRESS CATALOG CARD NO. 88-3928

FIRST PUBLISHED IN 1988 BY VIKING PENGUIN INC. PUBLISHED SIMULTANEOUSLY IN CANADA.

THANKS TO SEÑORA NANCY PAULSEN

3 4 5 6 7 8 9 10

THIS BOOK IS FOR SARA AND SHOSHANA

HEY WILLY, SEE THE PYRAMIDS

by MAIRA KALMAN

ALORS LOUIE, WHAT TIME IS IT?

Viking

Sometimes,
in the middle of the night,
when it is dark,
I call to my sister:
"Lulu, Lulu, Lulu.
Wake up. I can't sleep.
Tell me stories."
"Oh no," says Lulu
from far away, "not again,"
and shuffles over
to my bed.

She wiggles around,
gets comfortable,
sinks in.

"How many?" she says.
"A million?" I say.
"No," she says.
"Five?" I say.
"OK, five."

And Lulu begins.

big story

A very big woman
in a red dress
walked down the street
with three cross-eyed dogs.

When the dogs saw a yellow car
they started to bark.
The barking woke Aunt Ida,
who immediately started to sing.
The singing woke Uncle Morris,
who immediately started
to dance.

green hat

The three cross-eyed dogs
felt hungry.
They went to a fancy restaurant
and got a good table.

At the restaurant
a woman in a green hat
took a picture of a man
in a blue suit
while flowers sat
on the table
and smelled so sweet.

tiny story

Four very tiny people
walked right by me
on the way to school.
No one knew
where they were going,
but they were
walking very fast
and carrying
little instruments.

fish story

In front of
blue mountains
and green mountains
a thin skinny man
saw fish flying up.

the story of the party

Aunt Ida had a party.
The whole family was there.

Mr. Zelikovitch brought his son,
the genius, who was always
eating herring and
reading books.
Sara, the beauty, sat in the
middle of the room
peeling apples.
Leon brought ten warm cakes
and Aunt Rose wore her bathing suit,
because she swims in the ocean
every day.

It was time
for the surprise.

"Please sit down,"
announced the man
in the red suit.
"I will sing a song
for you."

We clapped
and shouted bravo
and Jerome fell off his chair.

Am I sleeping?
Yes.
Am I dreaming?
Yes.
Did Mr. Zelikovitch bring his pet chicken?
Yes, he did.
Did Dada and Dudu wear hats?
Yes, pointy ones.
Did Maishel Shmelkin really forget
his pants?
Yes, it's true.
Could you tell me
more stories?

Shhh. Listen.

chicken story

A girl in a green dress
bought three oranges and a chicken
for dinner. Then she dressed
her brother neatly in red pants
and a little blue shirt. They
danced and danced until it
was late.

tiptoe story

Aunt Ida and Uncle Morris had a dog
named Max.
Max wanted to live in Paris
and be a poet.
In the evening,
Max would tiptoe
down the hall, with a suitcase,
trying to sneak out of the house.
Ida would say to Morris,
"Quick, Morris,
catch the dog."

the poem of max

Max felt blue,
He went to the café
and ordered black coffee and biscuits.
He wrote down a poem
that went like this.

"Dig that boy
with the box
on his head.
Is he buying bread?
Is his name Fred?
And that tall noodle woman
with the polka-dot shoes—
have you ever seen
a nose so red?"

green face

My cousin Ervin
has a green face
and orange hair.
He is a scientist
and he told me about germs
and about something
that is called nothing.
His mother has very small ears
but she hears everything.

"What is nothing?" I ask.

"Nothing is when you are given
a very small portion of ice cream
by an adult,
and you look at the plate
and at the adult
and you ask for more
and the adult says
you have a huge portion
and you say
'That's it? That's nothing.'
"And that is nothing," says Lulu.

"I love Max the dog
and I will take him to Paris one day."

"I want to go to sleep, Alexander."

"Just one more story."

"And then,
good
night."

A boy had a dream.

He had gone
on a trip
to a faraway place.
It was hot and sandy.
The evening was pink
and far-off music
was in the air.
His uncle turned to him
and with a sweep of his arm, said,
"Hey Willy,
see the pyramids."

"The end," Lulu whispers.
I think I am asleep.
Then Lulu shuffles back
to her bed
and we both sink in
and see flying chairs
and green hats
and pink things
and sink some and
slowly sink
into sleep.

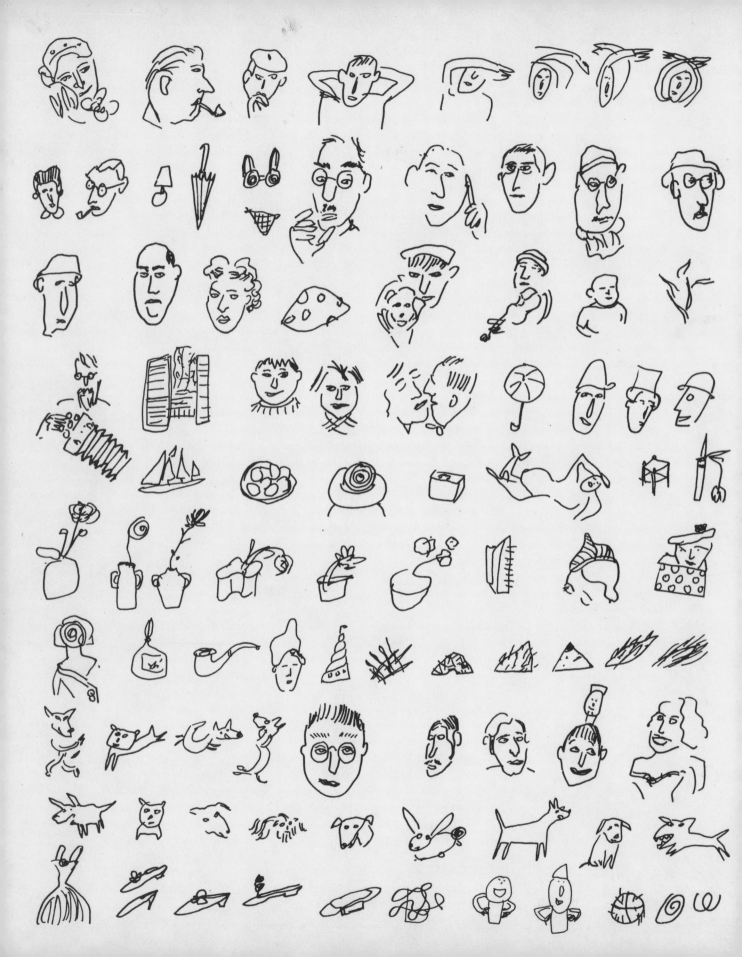